To the keeper of this book—it's time for you to visit the magical kingdom waiting within. Believe in yourself—that will give you wings to fly!

To Anne Clark, my agent,
with so much thanks for her support and
encouragement whilst I was writing
The Magical Kingdom of Birds series

Illustrated by Rosie Butcher and Hannah McCaffery,
based on original artwork by Rosie Butcher

OXFORD
UNIVERSITY PRESS

Great Clarendon Street, Oxford OX2 6DP
Oxford University Press is a department of the University of Oxford.
It furthers the University's objective of excellence in research, scholarship,
and education by publishing worldwide. Oxford is a registered trade mark of
Oxford University Press in the UK and in certain other countries

Text copyright © Anne Booth 2020
Illustrations copyright © Rosie Butcher 2020
The moral rights of the author have been asserted
Database right Oxford University Press (maker)

First published 2020

British Library Cataloguing in Publication Data

Data available

ISBN: 978-0-19-276631-1

1 3 5 7 9 10 8 6 4 2

Printed in Great Britain
Paper used in the production of this book is a natural,
recyclable product made from wood grown in sustainable forests.
The manufacturing process conforms to the environmental
regulations of the country of origin.

Magical Kingdom of Birds
The Flamingo Party

ANNE BOOTH

Illustrated by Rosie Butcher

OXFORD
UNIVERSITY PRESS

Chapter One

It was Sunday afternoon. Maya and her friends Theo and Saffron had all gone swimming together and were having hot chocolate back at Maya's house. Maya loved going swimming with her friends and they were all feeling happily tired and laughing about lots of things together.

'Mum and Dad have invited Alicia

1

and her parents over for dinner tonight,' said Saffron, as she squirted cream on her hot chocolate. 'They want to talk to them about starting a Carnival in our town, with a big musical parade with decorated floats and dancing. Alicia's mum was talking to my mum at ballet about it. Apparently they organized one every year in the town they used to live in.'

'A carnival parade sounds such fun,' said Maya. 'I've seen decorated floats and carnival costumes. Here, Dad says we can each have a chocolate flake to put in the cream.'

Theo took a big slurp of his hot chocolate and ended up with a dollop of cream on his nose, which made them laugh. Maya took a noisy slurp of hers and got a dollop on her nose too. They both looked very funny.

'Honestly! You two!' laughed Saffron, who was being very neat and using a spoon.

'Is Alicia the new girl in your class? The one you like so much, Saffron?' asked Theo, squirting more cream on his hot chocolate and letting Maya put a chocolate flake in his drink too.

'We all like her, don't we Maya?' said Saffron. 'Alicia is so friendly and smiley. I see her at ballet and she is so good. Alicia is good at everything really.'

'I bet she isn't as good as Maya at swimming and horse riding,' said Theo, loyally.

'Well, anyway, I thought that maybe you could come over after dinner and see her photographs of the carnival, Maya. Alicia danced at the front of the procession in her town's carnival and she said her costume was amazing. I bet she looked beautiful. Do you want to

4

come over and see her pictures, Maya?'

'No, I'm a bit too tired,' said Maya, suddenly feeling a bit miserable.

'Oh, that's a shame,' Saffron said, disappointed. 'I thought it would be nice for Alicia to get to know you, and I told her I was sure you would love to see her photos and would have brilliant ideas for what we could do for the carnival. She is so nice, Maya. I've been talking to her at ballet and I think she could be a real best friend for us.'

I don't want another best friend, thought Maya. She didn't want to share Saffron with anyone else. If Alicia was so friendly and pretty and good at everything, what if Saffron decided she preferred Alicia?

'I can't dance like Alicia,' said Maya.

'Dancing isn't the only thing people do in a carnival, anyway,' said Saffron. 'There's lots of music and floats and costumes too. That's what I want us to plan, not dancing. Come on, Maya. It's hard being a new girl. You were so nice to me and Theo when we moved here— why can't you be nice to Alicia?'

'Sorry, I haven't got time to come over later,' said Maya, grumpily, not answering Saffron's question. They were in her room, and Saffron looked around it at all the bird books and pictures, and the binoculars and satchel over her chair.

'Well, I don't know what you are doing, but if you finish early, please, please come over tonight Maya. I really want us all to be friends. I told Alicia you will have brilliant ideas for our costumes and our float.'

'What about two is company, three is a crowd?' muttered Maya.

'What about the Three Musketeers—

all for one and one for all?' said Saffron, crossly. 'And you never say that when Theo, you and I do things.'

'That's different,' said Maya.

'I don't think it is. I think you are just being mean and silly,' snapped Saffron, which was very unlike her. She was normally such a kind and encouraging person.

'I'll let myself out,' said Saffron. 'Come on Theo.' Maya didn't bother to wheel herself down the corridor to say goodbye.

Maya heard the front door shut and

suddenly felt really miserable. Lauren,

her big sister, was away at university,

and Penny, her stepmother, and her dad were planning to watch a boring television programme after dinner, all about buying houses. It would have been fun to have gone over to play with Saffron and Theo.

'Why did Alicia have to move here and spoil everything? Saffron is MY best friend. She likes ME best,' said Maya. She tried not to think about Saffron and Alicia having fun together without her, planning that silly carnival, and felt hot prickly tears rise up in her eyes. She blinked them angrily away.

Maya looked out at the garden to see if there were any birds to cheer her up. It was spring, and she loved seeing all the busy birds gathering things for their nests.

Suddenly she saw a flash of black and white, and her spirits lifted. It was a magpie. Maybe it was a sign that she should open her satchel and get out the special colouring book her mother had left her before she had died. Nobody knew, but the colouring book and the pencils which came with it were magic, and if a new picture appeared in it, and

11

Maya coloured it in, she would immediately be taken to the Magical Kingdom of Birds to have an adventure with her dear friends Willow, a fairy princess, and Patch, a talking magpie.

In the Magical Kingdom Maya had a very important job—she was the Keeper of the Book, and helped Willow and Patch defeat the plans of Willow's wicked Uncle Astor. Princess Willow should be the ruler of the Magical Kingdom, but Willow's uncle had destroyed her royal feathered cloak and taken over the kingdom himself.

Maya took out the book. It was so beautiful that it always made her feel amazed that it was really hers. The cover was deep blue, and there were tiny golden birds all over it, back and front. Maya recognized nearly all of them: hummingbirds and fairy-wrens and swans and snowy owls and snow geese and eagles and lyrebirds and songbirds and a cheeky magpie, which seemed to wink at her.

'Patch!' Maya laughed out loud.

And then suddenly, unexpectedly, the cover itself changed. All the golden birds disappeared, leaving only a blue cover, which became like lake water with white clouds reflected in it. Then, from the bottom left hand corner, a tiny, single, bright pink flamingo waded into the lake with its long jointed legs. Its long neck and head with its ruby-red eyes and hooked black beak moved from side to side, then it dipped its head right into the water to feed. It lifted its head again, opened its wings, and there was a flash of crimson and black from its undersides.

Maya watched, fascinated, as another

flamingo stepped on to the cover, as if from the side of a stage, and then another, and another, until there was a whole line of flamingos pressed closely up against each other, red eyes gleaming, marching together, moving their heads, bending their necks to preen their breast feathers, dipping down to feed, occasionally twisting their necks to touch bills with their neighbour, making heart shapes.

Maya was mesmerized as the cover filled with lines of marching pink flamingos, joining first from the left, and then from the right, moving up the cover until the whole book, from top to bottom, was covered with thousands of tiny birds. They moved in what looked like a graceful, choreographed dance, packed tightly together and yet moving as a group, still free to feed or preen or display their wings as they moved continuously along in lines, never bumping into each other.

All at once Maya's room itself seemed full of noise. The flamingos' calls, like scratchy honks, reminded her of geese, and Maya could hear the splashing of water and the beating of wings. She felt full of excitement and happiness, as if she was at a wonderful party.

'I think this must be what they call a flamboyance of flamingos,' she said, staring at the cover. 'I wish I were there.'

And for a moment she was, looking down over an incredible scene. She was flying over a big blue lake, but the main colour was pink, and flamingos were everywhere, preening and displaying and marching together and filling the air with excited calls.

Then all at once the scene disappeared

and Maya was sitting alone in her quiet room. The cover of the book in her hands had its usual tiny golden birds all over it. Outside, the garden was green.

'Did that really happen?' said Maya to herself, but then she heard a tapping at the window and looked out at the garden to see a magpie, its head cocked.

'There must be a new picture in the book. I must be needed back in the Magical Kingdom of Birds!' Maya said, her heart beating faster. 'I cannot wait!'

She opened the book, and, sure enough, there was a new picture to colour in, but the strangest one Maya had ever seen.

The picture wasn't of the flamboyance at all. It looked more like the surface of the moon, with lots of mounds, looking like small craters with raised edges. The odd thing was that there was a solitary sad looking adult flamingo beside one, where a little flamingo chick was perched on top, its long legs dangling over the side.

'What are flamingos doing on the moon?' said Maya, surprised.

Maya opened her bag to get her

pencils, and the pink, black, red, and grey all rolled towards her. She coloured in the flamingo and her chick, but the magic pencils wouldn't let her use any more colours or fill in the white.

'This is so strange,' Maya said to herself. 'It's so white. It almost looks like ice, but flamingos don't live in cold places, and this looks so much like the moon. What is going on? No wonder Willow needs me.'

And then a glittering pink feather appeared in front of her eyes, and another, and another, first moving in

lines like the flamingos had done, but
then whirling around her like confetti,
or snow in a snow globe. She was caught
up in the magic and Maya found herself
lifted up and tumbling through the air
towards the Magical Kingdom of Birds.
A new adventure was about to begin!

Chapter Two

Maya opened her eyes. The first thing she noticed was that it was very, very hot. She was outside, the book in a bag over her shoulders, and was sitting on a white, hard, mound. The sky above was very blue and, looking down, she realized that what she'd thought was ice in the picture, was something else. It was gritty, and looked like salt.

It was very, very quiet. The only sound was the gentle scratchy voice of a flamingo and the answering higher-pitched calls of a chick sat on a nearby mound as they talked together.

'I want to join the others, Mummy,' the chick was saying.

'I know. Soon. Don't worry, darling Oscar,' said the adult. She turned to look at Maya. 'Who are you?' she said, in a surprised voice, but before Maya could answer, there was a flapping of wings and a familiar sight met her eyes.

Princess Willow, and Patch the talking magpie, were both flying towards them.

'Greetings, Princess Willow and Patch,' said the adult, bowing.

'It's Princess Willow! It's Princess Willow!' shouted Oscar delightedly.

'Hush, my darling!' her mother said.

'And Patch the magnificent magpie,' grumbled Patch as he landed and perched on the mound on the other side of Maya.

'Hello Maya!' called Patch. 'Greetings, Vanessa!'

'Hello Maya, hello Vanessa!' called

24

Willow. She flew over and hovered as she passed Maya a quiver holding two specially woven willow sticks. 'Patch thought you would be here, so he insisted on getting his harness on and bringing your sticks. Ow! That's hot!' said Willow as her bare feet touched the ground. 'Budge up Maya,' and she flew up to the mound to sit next to her.

'That's why we build our nests above the ground,' said Vanessa. 'It's cooler up there.'

'This is a nest?' said Maya.

'Yes, we make them from salty lake

mud and they bake in the heat,' explained Vanessa. 'We lay an egg on the mound, and then both parents take turns to hatch the egg out.'

'That's me!' said the little flamingo, cheerfully. 'I'm Oscar! Who are you?'

'Vanessa and Oscar, please meet Maya, the Keeper of the Book,' said Willow.

'Oh dear,' said Vanessa, looking anxious. 'That means there must be a problem. I know that the Keeper of the Book only comes when there is trouble.'

'Yes, but she always helps us sort it

27

out,' said Willow, reassuringly. 'Now, Vanessa, please tell us where all the other flamingos are, and why you are alone here.'

'The other flamingos have flown ahead with Lord Astor, to his lake,' said Vanessa. 'He said it was the best lake, and would have the most food for us. The other young flamingos are walking there with their flamingo guardians, but Oscar wasn't quite strong enough, so his father and I are taking turns to feed him up a bit more to get him strong.'

They heard a beating of wings and a

large and beautiful male pink flamingo landed, stretching his wings to show a flash of red and black.

He walked over to Oscar, who opened his beak, and he poured a red liquid from his beak into Oscar's. Then he and Vanessa touched bills affectionately.

'Greetings to you, Idris,' said Princess Willow.

The flamingo bowed gracefully.

'Some parrots told me they saw lots of flamingos flying with Lord Astor, and they were worried, because they know my uncle is not to be trusted,' said Willow. 'Someone told me you were still here, Vanessa and Idris, so I thought, as you are the leading flamingos, that there must be a problem.'

'I knew there was a problem,' said Patch, triumphantly to Maya. 'And I said to Princess Willow, if there is trouble, there will be Maya, so we'd better get the harness on and bring her sticks.'

'I don't know how to take that,' said Maya. 'I don't like you always having to be in trouble before I can visit.'

'I'm glad you're here, anyway,' said Patch, gruffly.

'He saw us all in our flamboyance, parading and displaying on our lake when we were pairing up and choosing mates,' said Vanessa, who was now sitting on the mound with Oscar tucked under her wing. 'It was before your father and I met, and I laid your egg, Oscar,' she said lovingly, looking down at her chick.

'The book cover showed me that!' said Maya. 'You all looked amazing!'

'Thank you,' said Idris. 'Lord Astor saw us and said his lake was perfect for us, and that he wanted us to come and perform in a big carnival at his castle in honour of you, Princess Willow, as a surprise. He said that he would invite all the birds from all over the kingdom to come and watch. We wouldn't normally march and parade again, but as it was for you, Princess Willow, we all agreed, because we love you.'

'I want to be in the carnival for Princess Willow!' said Oscar. 'I love you Princess Willow!'

He climbed out from under his mother and out of the nest and stood unsteadily on the salt.

'Look! I'm flying!' he said, jumping up and down, but his little downy feathers and tiny wings weren't quite strong enough. Maya thought he looked very sweet.

'Your feathers will grow in time,' said Vanessa, fondly. 'That's why I tell you to keep preening and grooming to encourage your adult feathers to grow.'

'I do feel concerned now that we are apart from the others,' said Idris. 'We flamingos always stay together. Lord Astor wanted us to leave earlier than we normally do at this time of year. Just a few days more would have been better for Oscar and some of the other little ones. They must be exhausted. At least he said his lake is near, and full of food.'

'We think it is nearly time for Oscar

for join the other young ones and feed himself, filtering algae and brine shrimp from the mud of the marsh,' said Vanessa.

'Daddy and Mummy say that all the little flamingos have lots of fun together all day, and they come back to be with us at night,' said Oscar, excitedly. 'I want to go to the lake NOW.'

'Hmm, I'm a bit worried,' said Willow. 'I know the palace lake, and I have never seen flamingos feed there. There are no marshes around it either.'

'That's not good,' said Idris, worriedly. 'We flamingos need to eat a special diet.

We filter algae through our beaks That's the reason we are pink.'

'My beak is going to get more and more curved and I'm going to eat lots and lots and be the pinkest flamingo in the WORLD,' boasted Oscar. He jumped up and down excitedly but wobbled and nearly fell into a big salt puddle. Luckily Maya quickly put out one of her sticks and stopped him in time.

'Thank you!' said Vanessa. 'The salt puddles are a big worry now he is walking —if he falls in one and wet salt gets on his legs and dries and hardens it will be hard for him to walk. It will be a relief to get away to the lake.'

Oscar had got a bit of a fright and was crying. 'I don't like the salt. I want to go to the lake with the others,' he said, as Willow gave him a cuddle.

'Maya, could you hold on to Oscar if he sat on my back?' said Patch.

'Of course,' said Maya. So she used her sticks and went over to Patch, who crouched down so she could climb up on to his back, as she normally did. She settled herself with her bag and Vanessa and Willow helped Oscar onto Patch.

Oscar's legs were so long it was a bit difficult at first for Patch to move his wings to fly, so Oscar had to sit backwards facing Maya, his legs on either side whilst Maya cuddled him close, and then Patch soared up into the air.

They flew over a wide expanse of white salt, and up in the air it was clear that around the edges of the big salt island was blue lake water. Willow flew in front and Vanessa and Idris flew beside them, their extended bodies long and elegant, their pink feathers looking beautiful against the blue sky.

Oscar was a very friendly little flamingo and didn't seem to mind not facing the direction they were going. He had forgotten his recent fright and liked looking up into Maya's face and chatting.

'I'm going to make lots of new friends

at the carnival,' he confided. 'When I meet my friend Belinda, again, she will have made new friends in the line and then they will be MY friends too and we are going to have lots of fun together.'

Maya felt a bit ashamed of how cross she had been with Saffron for being kind to Alicia. Oscar wasn't jealous—he loved that his friend was making new friends.

'I can't see any long line of young flamingos and their guardians,' said Vanessa, worriedly. 'They seem to have completely disappeared.'

'Maybe they have arrived at the castle

40

already,' said Willow, turning back to reassure her. 'It's not a long journey.'

They flew over green fields and meandering rivers, Oscar chatting all the time.

'Why have you got a big bag?' asked Oscar.

'Because it has got a big book and pencils in it,' said Maya.

'Why?' asked Oscar.

'Well because it is a magic book, and I am the Keeper of the Book because my mother gave it to me,' said Maya.

'Why?' asked Oscar.

'I'm sorry,' said Vanessa, flying alongside. 'Oscar asks a lot of questions and he doesn't know when to stop.'

'I don't mind,' said Maya, but she wished she had an answer to give her little flamingo friend. Why had her mother owned the book and pencils, and why had she left them to Maya? Who could tell her? Would she ever know?

Chapter
Three

It wasn't long before they saw the turrets
of the castle in the distance, and forests
and mountains behind it.

As they got closer they heard a hubbub
and they saw a huge crowd of pale pink
flamingos walking in the lake, their
reflections in the blue lake pale pink as
well. It looked pretty, but the flamingos

did not seem very happy. They were dipping their heads in the water and lifting them up again and shaking them.

'What's happening?' asked Idris, as they flew down low above them. 'Why are you so pale?'

'There is no food in the lake for us to eat,' said one. 'Blaise and Rose have gone to complain. We are getting paler and weaker by the minute.'

They flew on to the shore, where they found Lord Astor arguing with a very old flamingo and a tall, elegant boy fairy dressed in pink.

'It is Blaise, the flamingo fairy, and Rose, the oldest flamingo of all,' Willow said, flying next to Maya and Patch and Oscar.

'Uncle!' cried Willow, flying in and standing, hands on hips, in front of Lord Astor. 'What are you doing?'

'Niece! I am glad you are here!' said Lord Astor. 'I'm having a carnival. The best carnival EVER. I've summoned birds here from all over the country, and I'm going to be the Carnival King. The flamingos have given me their best pink feathers and my guards are making a MAGNIFICENT headdress for me. It will be SO much better than your silly feathered cloak was.'

'Princess Willow,' said Blaise, bowing

low. 'The flamingos only agreed to take part in the carnival because they thought it was for you, and they only gave him feathers because he has locked up their children in the castle. He says he won't let them out until he is wearing his carnival headdress.'

'Uncle!' said Willow, shocked.

'I could never imagine a true ruler of the Magical Kingdom of Birds doing this,' said Rose.

'What?' said Lord Astor, sulkily. 'I have laid on an AMAZING party for them in the castle. They have jellies and cake and ice cream and pink wafer biscuits. They can come out when my headdress is ready. I don't want their parents to fly away in case I need more feathers. But the guards have told me they have finished my headdress anyway, so you can stop fussing, niece.' He clapped his hands and the guards brought out a huge headdress—but it wasn't pink but a greyish white.

'WHAT?' screamed Lord Astor, his face red with fury. 'How DARE you. I gave you pink flamingo feathers.'

'It wasn't our fault. They turned grey

when we made the headdress,' said the bravest guard.

'You will be punished for this!' Lord Astor started shouting at the flamingos on the lake. 'I will NEVER let your young flamingos go.'

The pale flamingos, hearing this, started swaying and honking in distress, and Blaise and Rose and Idris and Vanessa rushed to be with them.

Princess Willow was angrier than Maya had ever seen her

'Stop this right now!' she shouted. 'How can you be so ignorant, Uncle? Of course the flamingo feathers in the headdress aren't pink. They are only pink when they are on the flamingos' bodies, because they get the colour from brine shrimp, or the algae they eat in the lakes. Look how pale and weak they are getting because you lied to them about the palace lake being full of food. And how COULD you give baby flamingos the wrong food? That could make them very, very ill. Let me in immediately. Fairy guards, stand aside. You should be ashamed of yourself, Uncle. You have done bad things in the past, but I think this is the worst. You are a very bad fairy.'

She glared so hard at her uncle he looked a bit scared. He sulkily nodded and the fairy guards opened the doors to the dining hall, where the party had been laid out. They all rushed in. There were bright balloons and streamers and big party banners saying 'Astor is the best' and 'Astor is amazing' on the walls, but the scene was very miserable. The baby flamingos were gathered together in a corner and looked very sick and scared.

'It's my friend Belinda!'

Oscar rushed towards two little

flamingos who were looking very sorry
for themselves.

'We don't like the cake, Oscar. We
don't like this party. We want our
mummies and daddies!' Belinda cried.

'Of course you do,' soothed Willow.

'Don't worry. I'm so glad you didn't eat much. We'll have you out of here in no time. Fairy guards—help these poor little things out and bring them back to their parents. I've never heard of fairies from the Magical Kingdom of Birds feeding such dangerous stuff to birds before. You should all be ashamed of yourselves.'

The fairy guards, who did look very ashamed now, helped Willow, Maya, Patch, and Oscar bring all the young flamingos out into the sun, but as they led the last ones out, there were lots of splashing noises, one after the other, and everyone watched, appalled, as the adult pink flamingos started fainting, one after the other, into the shallow, clear water of the palace lake.

'Quick! Get everyone you can out of the water immediately, and hold the heads up of those who have already fainted!' commanded Willow, and the horrified palace guards rushed to help.

Rose, Vanessa, and Idris helped as many flamingos as they could out of the water to the shore, where they collapsed, pale and weak. Blaise, Willow, Maya, and Patch organized the young flamingos and the fairy guards to stand in the shallows and hold the heads up of the ones who had fainted in the water, and then, when they were ready, they helped them up to the shore.

'What have you done, Uncle?' cried Willow. 'Maya, what can we do to put this right?'

'I'm so sorry!' cried Lord Astor, finally truly appalled at what he had done, and he ran off, crying, into the castle.

'Oh, if only my uncle hadn't destroyed the feathered cloak!' said Willow in distress.

Maya opened the book to see what it said, but there was no new page to help her. It was up to her. She suddenly had an idea.

'If you had the feathered cloak, what would you do?'

'I would put on the cloak, clap my hands three times and issue the special Royal Emergency command every royal child is taught,' said Willow.

'Clap your hands and say the words anyway,' said Maya. 'Go on, Willow.'

Willow clapped her hands three times and called out in a clear voice:

'Birds of the air, of land and sea,

I now summon you to me.

Come at once, without delay,

Fairies too, do what I say.'

And everything changed.

Chapter Four

There was an overpowering rushing
sound of beating wings, and birds and
fairies of all shapes and sizes and colours
appeared in the air from everywhere.
Even penguins and other flightless birds
were being carried by their fairies, in
their arms or on their backs. Maya
recognized friends she had met and made

over many adventures.

'How . . . how did that happen?' said Willow, astonished as the birds and fairies hovered expectantly, waiting for her next command.

'Don't you see—you already are the true Queen of the Magical Kingdom of Birds!' said Maya. 'You don't need a feathered cloak or fine clothes or even a palace to take your place as the true ruler,' said Maya. 'You just need to be yourself and love them and know them and want to serve them. All the adventures we have had together have shown me how brave and unselfish you are, and how you always put the birds first. That's why you had the power to summon them.'

'What do we do now?' said Willow.

'Well, what do the flamingos need?'

'They need to drink from a lake which has the food they need,' said Willow. 'But they are too weak to fly there.'

'So we go to the lake and bring the food to them!' said Blaise, the flamingo fairy, excitedly.

'Inside the castle there are glasses and goblets and bowls and cups and buckets and saucepans,' said Willow. 'I will call each bird group and their fairies in turn and send them off to get something they can carry water in.'

Once Willow took command everything got better. Hummingbirds flew back and forth to the flamingo lake with egg cups, golden eagles with saucepans, and pelicans carried water back to the flamingos in their huge beaks. The fairies helped the poorly flamingos lift their heads and dip them into buckets of lake water to feed, until they felt well enough to stand.

'Now I want all the birds to accompany the flamingos back to their lake, and to fly close beside them and support them if they are weak,' commanded Willow. 'Fairies—including my uncle's guards— I want you all to help carry the young

birds who cannot fly. They are still too weak to walk to the marshes.'

'Yes, Queen Willow, ruler of the kingdom,' they all called joyfully, and with a massive fluttering of wings and a loud, last din of birdsong and calls, suddenly the lake and shore were empty.

'We'd better follow and make sure everything goes smoothly,' said Willow. 'Even when we get back to the lake, I fear the weak flamingos will take time to recover and get their colour back.'

'Can we stay here and talk for a minute?' said Maya to Patch, quietly.

'Of course,' said Patch.

'We'll follow on soon,' said Maya.

'Of course! See you there!' called Willow back over her shoulder, as she and Blaise carried Oscar, and Rose flew beside them.

'Whee! This is fun!' called Oscar, happily.

Maya waited until they'd disappeared over the horizon and then turned to Patch.

'Patch, we didn't need the book to save the flamingos, and Willow didn't need her feathered cloak to be Queen, as she had the power inside all along.'

'But you helped her to discover that,' said Patch.

'Yes, but now I have, and if there are no new pictures, am I needed any more as the Keeper of the Book? Is this my last visit to the Magical Kingdom?' Maya tried not to cry, but her voice wobbled.

'Open the book again and see if it tells you,' said Patch, speaking more gently than Maya had ever heard him.

She opened it again, and there was a picture.

'Oh no!' she said. 'Not him! Ugh!'

It was a picture of the back of Lord Astor, inside the castle, staring at the throne.

'I'm not that keen on him either,' said Patch, 'but I think we need to listen to the book.'

A red pencil jumped into her hands, and she started colouring in his cloak anyway, and immediately she and Patch were in the castle, and Lord Astor was standing there, just as in the picture.

Lord Astor turned to see them, and his face was wet with tears.

'I am so, so sorry,' he said. 'What can I do to put things right?'

Suddenly, the book Maya was holding flew out of her grasp, across the room and into Lord Astor's hands.

Lord Astor looked amazed and a little frightened to find himself holding it. Maya felt her heart break a little to see him hold her book, but she knew deep

down something right was happening.

Lord Astor clutched the book in his arms and sank down to the floor, sobbing, and Maya found herself rushing forward to comfort him.

'I can't believe I am holding it at last,' he wept. 'Your mother said I could hold it, but I said that if I couldn't have it for my own I didn't want it, and if she didn't give it to me to keep, I wouldn't be her friend. I thought that if she really loved me the way she said she did, she would give me her book and promise to only be friends with me.'

'You knew my mother?' said Maya, amazed.

'Yes, I recognized you as soon as I saw you,' said Willow's uncle. 'You look so like her, but I didn't want to admit it. She was my best friend when I was a young fairy, but I got jealous when she made friends with my sister too, and I stopped talking to her, though she pleaded with me to be friends all together. I was so angry I swore to take my revenge on my sister and her family. But I've never had a friend since and I'm so lonely.'

He cried and cried.

'I should have listened to your lovely mother. I've hurt the Magical Kingdom of Birds so much. I've been so bad. How can I put things right?'

'Let's look in the book together,' said Maya.

'Really?' said Astor.

Maya gave him a hug and nodded. He wiped his eyes with his sleeve, and then the book opened.

It was the best picture of all. There was a double page spread of a smiling Queen Willow wearing her feathered cloak and a crown, surrounded by happy, bright pink flamingos and birds of every kind.

'How can she be wearing the feathered cloak if you destroyed it?' said Maya.

Astor looked a bit embarrassed. 'I didn't exactly destroy it,' he admitted sheepishly. 'I didn't want to tell Willow that it came apart when I tried to put it on,

and all the feathers flew away from me.'

'So if the picture is coloured in, maybe this picture will come true and the cloak will re-make itself and come back,' said Patch, looking over their shoulders.

'It's the biggest and most complicated picture the book has shown me,' said

Maya. 'There are so many different feathers in the cloak, and so many birds to colour in. It will take ages.'

'Please let me help,' said Lord Astor, and as he said that, a pink pencil jumped out of Maya's bag and into his hands.

'I think the book agrees!' laughed Maya, surprised at how much she liked Willow's uncle now. She sighed. He had lost his best friend because of jealousy. She mustn't do the same. As soon as she returned home she would go over to Saffron and Theo's and make friends with Alicia.

They both lay on their tummies on
the soft rug of the throne room, and with

the help of the magical pencils, coloured in the picture together, Patch encouraging them. As they coloured in, Lord Astor told Patch and Maya lots of funny stories about his childhood and his sister, Willow's mother, and his friendship with Maya's mum. It made Maya sad and happy and proud at the same time to hear all these stories about the mum she couldn't remember, and Lord Astor cried and laughed as he told them. This picture was the most beautiful in the book, glowing with colour. And as Maya put the last finishing touches on the cloak, and Lord Astor coloured the last pink flamingo wing, suddenly they were all in the scene itself.

'Maya! Look! The feathered cloak and the crown have appeared out of nowhere!' said Willow, her face radiant. 'And all the adult flamingos are suddenly completely pink and well again!'

'Your uncle and I coloured in the book together,' said Maya, showing the page to Willow.

'I am so sorry, niece, and I renounce all claim to the throne,' said Astor, kneeling down in front of her. 'Please forgive me for all I did to you and your family and birds. You are truly the rightful ruler of the Magical Kingdom of Birds, and I am just a horrible, jealous person.'

'No you're not,' said Maya. 'You were my mother's friend, and she loved you, and now you are my friend too.'

'Really?' said Lord Astor. His face lit up. He looked so relieved, and happier than she had ever seen him.

'Yes, really,' said Maya. She was surprised to hear herself say it, but she realized she truly meant it. Lord Astor was, at last, properly sorry for all the bad things he had done, and for the jealousy which had caused all the problems.

'Please forgive me, niece Willow, Queen of the Magical Kingdom, and Maya, Patch, and all the birds I have hurt,' said Lord Astor, humbly. 'I will never bother you again.'

Queen Willow frowned for a moment, looking beautiful and regal in her crown and cloak.

'You promise to love and help all the fairies and birds in the kingdom from now on, and be a true friend to us all?'

'That's what I want to do more than anything,' said Lord Astor, and it was clear to everyone that he was truly sorry.

'Then of course I forgive you, Uncle! You must stay here and be a friend to us all—don't you agree, birds and fairies?' And the air was full of happy, forgiving birdsong and calls and fairy cheers from everyone else, including the fairy guards.

'Oh thank you, thank you,' said Lord Astor as Willow hugged him. 'This is the happiest day of my life!'

'Well, in that case,' said Queen

Willow, beaming at the bright pink flamingos, 'I think it is time for that party!'

Chapter Five

The lakeside carnival in honour of Queen Willow's coronation and Lord Astor was the most amazing party Maya had ever been to. It was so colourful and noisy and exciting.

Birds were singing and drumming and creating all sorts of music. Baby birds of all types were playing games, others were soaring and diving in the air, and swimming in the sea, and everywhere Maya looked, she could see birds dancing. Some were elegantly waltzing, some doing wild feather waving, strutting dances, others dancing in circles.

'Hello Maya!' cried a group of gorgeous hummingbirds, and she found herself hugged by a little golden fairy.

'Hello Honeysuckle!' Maya said, delightedly. 'Hello Little Bee!'

All the birds and fairies she had ever met came and hugged her. It was so lovely to catch up with them and hear how things were going. She felt so proud she had helped so many, and she was so impressed by how they had all forgiven Lord Astor. She could see him being given lake rides by the swans, or playing his flute in the songbird band. He was totally accepted and his face was beaming with joy.

'Maya!' said Rose, the flamingo. 'It's time! Climb on my back!' Rose bent down so that Maya could lean on her sticks and take her seat on Rose's pink feathered back. There was no harness, but Rose's feathers sank down under Maya's weight so it felt safe and cosy, almost like sitting in a nest, even when Rose began to move. She marched slowly over to Idris.

'It's marching time!' Rose laughed.

Idris began to sway. 'Queen Willow! Sit on my back,' he called.

'Can I come too, Daddy?' said Oscar.

'Of course, if Queen Willow can hold you,' he said, smiling down at his excited son.

'Come up and have a cuddle and a ride,' said Willow flying down and gathering up Oscar in her arms, and settling them both on Idris's back. 'This is fun!'

They marched closely together over to Vanessa.

'So it is time?' she said. 'Come, my magpie friend, sit on my back and we'll show you how flamboyant we can be together!'

One by one the other flamingos noticed what was happening, and joined the march. Lord Astor in his band noticed, and he and the birds and fairies flew over and perched on the flamingos backs, and carried on playing their instruments. More and more flamingos

joined in until there were thousands of them marching, dancing in perfect rhythm to the music, moving their necks and heads and displaying their wings. It was stupendous.

Maya, swaying on Rose's back, looked over and saw Willow and Oscar, and Patch, and the joyful, flute-playing Lord Astor, and she couldn't remember ever feeling so happy. She couldn't believe she was actually part of the flamboyance! All types of birds joined the march or made up their own dances in the air or on the ground or on the lake. Elegant swans and geese marched, whilst penguins waddled or dived with kingfishers in time to the music. She saw birds of paradise dancing with eagles, and owls dancing with peacocks. Every type of bird she could think of was dancing and having fun in their own way, or hovering just to watch the amazing flamingo dancing.

Eventually, after hours and hours, Vanessa and Idris and Rose flew up into the air to signal the end of the dancing, and the lines broke up with much shaking of feathers and laughter.

Maya rode on Rose's back to the front

of the palace, where Willow, Patch, and Lord Astor were waiting, sitting on the steps.

She slipped off Rose's back, and hugged her around the neck.

'Thank you, dear child, for saving the flamingos,' said Rose.

'Thank you, Rose, I will never forget you. Give my love to Blaise and Idris and Vanessa and Oscar,' said Maya. She could see them in the distance, Oscar's parents teaching him the steps for the next time, and Blaise hovering in the air beside them, laughing and clapping.

Maya took her sticks and walked over
to her dear friends.

'I'm going to look in the book one more time, but I'm afraid I know what I will see,' Maya said, lowering herself down and leaning against Patch's comforting feathered body.

She opened the book and they looked through it together. It allowed them to turn every page, and look back through all the adventures they had had as three friends. They exclaimed at the pictures and remembered all the ups and downs and the wonderful birds involved. Then Maya turned to the last page and it was totally clear that it *was* the last page. It was the picture she and Lord Astor had coloured in, but even more glowing and bright now, and beside the figure of Willow in her crown and cloak, were three more figures—Lord Astor, and

Patch, and Maya herself. And at the very bottom, in curly gold letters, was written

The End

Maya burst into tears.

'Don't cry, dear Maya,' said Willow. 'Remember our love will always be with you. We won't stay apart from you, even if we don't meet you in the pages of a book. We will come to you in your dreams whenever you want us to. Who knows what wonderful adventures are yet to come?'

'I can never thank you enough,' said Lord Astor. 'You have given me more than a kingdom—I have my niece and all the birds to love and take care of now. I won't let you down.'

'Go safely, Maya,' said Patch, his eyes bright. 'Don't think you're getting rid of me that easy. You will see me when you least expect me, and I will ALWAYS be your friend.'

Maya and Willow and Patch hugged. Lord Astor held back a little shyly, but Maya beckoned him to come and join in a big group goodbye.

'What about the book and the bag and the pencils? What should I do with them now?' said Maya, wiping her eyes.

'Do what your mother did,' said Patch. 'Keep it all safe, and one day, you will meet someone—it could be your own child, it could be a stranger, or a friend—but on that day you will know who is the next Keeper of the Book, and you will pass it on to them, or the book will find a way into their arms. Do not worry. Your job is done.'

'And don't worry, darling Maya, we WILL meet again soon,' said Willow, her beautiful brown kind eyes looking into Maya's, her black curls tickling her cheeks as she hugged her.

And then, suddenly, Maya was lifted up for one last time, surrounded by glittering feathers in all sizes and shapes, and tumbled magically back into her room at home, where it was still cool and quiet and green outside the window, and her friend Saffron was still across the road, waiting for her and hoping she would come.

Chapter Six

Carnival time had arrived and Maya's school had won first prize for their decorated float, which was leading the carnival procession through the town.

'What a brilliant idea you had, Maya,' said Alicia, standing next to her, beaming. They were the best of friends now.

'I don't know how on earth you

thought of the Magical Kingdom of Birds idea, but it looks FANTASTIC!' said Saffron, happily, giving Maya a hug. 'No wonder the Head chose it as our theme!'

All over the school's carnival float were bright paper and papier mâché models of birds and flowers and trees and even cardboard waves—children were dressed as hummingbirds and swans and fairy-wrens, owls and snow geese, flamingos and peacocks and puffins. Birdsong rang out from the speakers as they rode, and, in pride of place, because

she had thought of the winning idea,
Maya was seated on a model of a huge
black and white magpie.

'I can't believe we won first prize!' said Alicia, dressed in a pink flamingo costume and happily waving to the crowds.

'We get to choose the theme next time too,' said Saffron, who was dressed as a lovebird.

'Why are you just dressed as normal, Maya, with just a bag over your shoulders?' said Theo, Saffron's brother, who was dressed as a robin.

'I thought I'd dress up as the Keeper of the Book, who saves the Magical Kingdom of Birds from danger,' said Maya. She opened her satchel and showed Theo an ordinary colouring book full of pictures of birds, and some normal colouring pencils. 'If I colour in these, I get taken to a magical kingdom full of birds, and I save them from danger.'

Theo laughed. 'I love your stories, Maya!' he said.

Maya smiled to herself. She had hidden the real book and bag safely at the bottom of her wardrobe at home.

It was turning out to be such an amazing day, after months of excitement and fun and hard work preparing at school. The whole town had thrown itself into preparing for it. There was music, there were food and craft stalls everywhere along the road, and everyone was dancing and dressed up and having a wonderful time. Saffron had been right —Maya had come up with a brilliant idea for the Carnival, and Alicia was a lovely new friend.

'I can't wait to tell Patch and Willow how it all went,' thought Maya. She had seen her magical friends often in her dreams. The Kingdom was happy and contented now, and Maya loved meeting new birds and having fun with her old friends. Lord Astor had kept his promise and was being a wonderful uncle and was very popular and happy.

Willow and Patch were very interested in everything she told them about the Carnival. 'If you have a Magpie as the centrepiece you will DEFINITELY win,' Patch had boasted proudly.

'I'd like there to be something to remind you of me that day,' said Willow.

'Don't worry, I will be thinking of you all the time!' promised Maya. 'How can I not think of you when surrounded by birds?'

'Hey! Maya!' Maya looked over and saw her big sister Lauren running beside the float. 'Well done to everyone! It looks fabulous! Penny and Dad are waiting at the end for when you arrive. They are going to take photos, and a newspaper wants to interview you all. But Penny said I had to give you this parcel. It arrived on the doorstep and it says you MUST open it when you are on the float.'

Lauren passed it up to Theo and he passed it over to Maya. As soon as she saw it she felt a shiver of excitement.

It was soft and wrapped in coloured blue paper with lots of pictures of tiny golden birds all over it. Just like the cover of the book.

Maya felt her heart beat quickly.

There was a label, which in gold swirly letters simply said, 'To Maya, with all our love. To wear on the carnival float.'

'What beautiful paper!' said Saffron.

Maya opened it with trembling hands.

'Oh Maya! You have GOT to put that on,' said Alicia.

Maya took out the beautiful feathered

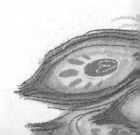

cloak and put it round her shoulders.

'You look wonderful!' said Saffron.

'That's amazing, Maya!' said Theo. 'Whoever sent that to you?'

'Friends I will see soon. Wonderful friends I'll tell you all about some day,' said Maya, and she smiled.

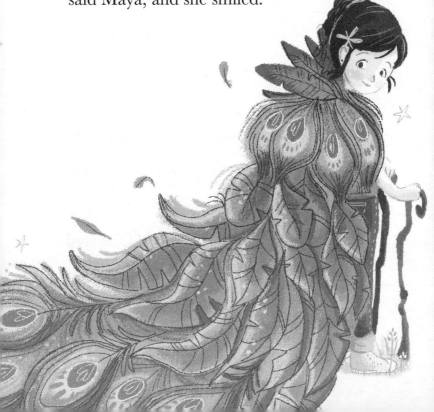

Acknowledgements

Thank you to Liz Cross, who commissioned this series originally, and to Clare Whitston and Debbie Sims for all your guidance, great ideas, and editing. I am so grateful I got to write this. I have had so much fun and I have learnt a lot about birds!

The documentary film I watched was called *The Crimson Wing: Mystery of the Flamingo*. This is a wonderful documentary but, as it is true to life, has some distressing scenes in it, and baby flamingos dying, so this needs to be taken into account when watching with children.

The main natural history book I read to help me write this was *Flamingo* by Caitlin R. Knight, published by Reaktion books.

Thank you to the wonderful illustrator Rosie Butcher — I am so lucky you illustrated this series — and to the brilliant designer Lizzie Robertson, who has made each book in the series look so beautiful inside and out, both on their own and put together on a shelf!

Thank you to Hannah Penny and all the sales and marketing people at OUP, and all the bloggers, librarians, and booksellers who have supported the series, and all who have left lovely reviews.

Thank you to the children and schools who have been so enthusiastic about Maya's adventures!

Thank you, as always, to my friend Helen Sole, teacher, play therapist, and athlete who played in the Great Britain sitting volleyball team, for her insight and advice throughout the series about Maya's problems with her legs and how I should write about them.

Thanks to my friends and neighbours who have been so supportive and bought so many books!

Thank you to my dogs Timmy and Ben, who did no writing or research, but were lovely company.

Thanks, as always, for all the support I have had from my children and my lovely husband Graeme. I've had such a lovely time writing this series.

About Anne

Every Christmas, Anne used to ask for a dog. She had to wait many years, but now she has two dogs, called Timmy and Ben. Timmy is a big, gentle golden retriever who loves people and food and is scared of cats. Ben is a small brown and white cavalier King Charles spaniel who is a bit like a cat because he curls up in the warmest places and bosses Timmy about. He snuffles and snorts quite a lot, and you can tell what he is feeling by the way he walks. He has a particularly pleased patter when he has stolen something he shouldn't have, which gives him away immediately. Anne lives in a village in Kent and is not afraid of spiders.

About Rosie

Rosie lives in a little town in East Yorkshire with her husband and daughter. She draws and paints by night, but by day she builds dens on the sofa, watches films about princesses, and attends tea parties. Rosie enjoys walking and having long conversations with her little girl, Penelope. They usually discuss important things like spider webs, birds, and prickly leaves.

Bird Fact File

Turn the page for information on the real-life birds that inspired this story.

Fun Facts

1. There are six species of flamingo.

2. The largest flamingo is the Greater flamingo, which stands at up to 1.5m tall.

3. The Lesser flamingo is the smallest species of flamingo, standing at 0.8m tall.

4. Because flamingos have long legs they can wade into quite deep water, but they are actually very good swimmers too.

5. Flamingos eat plankton, small crustaceans, algae, and other little organisms found in mudflats.

6. Flamingos feed upside down, putting their beaks, and sometimes their whole head, underwater.

7. Flamingos' beaks are specially shaped so that they can filter out food from the water.

8. Flamingos are pink because of a pigment called beta-carotene found in their food.

9. When kept in captivity flamingos often turn white because they have a different diet.

10. Flamingos live in a big group of up to several hundred birds. This keeps them safe from predators.

11. The feathers under their wings are black.

12. Flamingo chicks are born with grey and white feathers. They don't turn pink until they're one or two years old.

13. The name 'flamingo' comes from the Portuguese or Spanish word 'flamengo', meaning 'flame-coloured'.

14. Flamingos usually stand on one leg with the other one tucked in by their body. Nobody really knows why they do this! One theory is that it uses less energy to stand on one leg than two.

15. The wingspan of a flamingo can be as small as 90cm, or as big as 1.5m!

16. Males and females split into breeding groups of around 50 birds and all dance together.

17. Flamingos can live for a long time—the oldest known flamingo lived to be 83 years old!

18. Flamingos cannot bend their knees backwards, even though it looks like they can. That bit is actually their ankle!

19. Flamingos have a very poor sense of taste and no sense of smell!

Where do you find
flamingos?

You can find flamingos in the wild in southern Europe, parts of North and South America, Africa, the Middle East, and India!

Flamingo-pink cakes!

Ingredients:

- 100g caster sugar
- 100g butter, softened
- 100g self-raising flour
- 2 eggs
- 1 tsp vanilla extract
- Red food colouring

For the icing:

- 200g butter, softened
- 200g icing sugar
- Sprinkles
- Marshmallows

You will need:

- Weighing scales
- Bowl
- Sieve
- Whisk

- Fairy cake cases
- A 12-hole bun tin
- Piping bag
- A grown up helper

Step 1

Preheat the oven to
180°C/Fan 160°C/gas 4.

Step 2

Place fairy cake cases into
a 12-hole bun tin.

Step 3

Mix sugar and butter
together in the bowl, then
sift in the flour.

Step 4

Add the eggs and vanilla extract.

Step 5

Add a couple of drops of food colouring. Remember, a little goes a long way!

Step 6

Fill each paper case with the mixture.

Step 7

Bake for 15–20 minutes or until the cakes are well risen and golden brown.

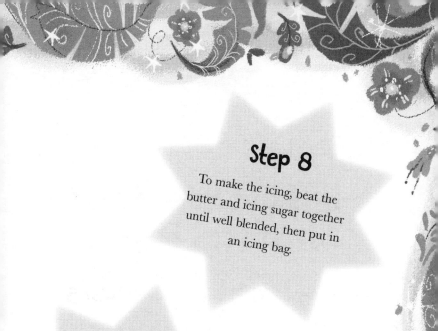

Step 8

To make the icing, beat the butter and icing sugar together until well blended, then put in an icing bag.

Step 9

Once the cakes are completely cool, pipe icing onto each cake and decorate.

Step 10

Enjoy!

Find out how Maya's adventures began in

The Sleepy Hummingbirds

When Maya receives a special colouring
book –*Magical Kingdom of Birds* – she is
transported to a beautiful realm filled with
magnificent birds and their fairy friends.
The kingdom is in trouble – evil Lord
Astor has a plan to capture and cage the
tiniest residents, the hummingbirds. Will
Maya be brave enough to save the day?

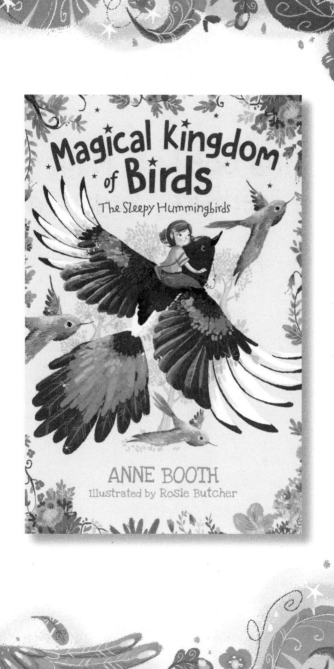

Magical Kingdom
of Birds
The Sleepy Hummingbirds

ANNE BOOTH

Illustrated by Rosie Butcher

Chapter One

Maya was sitting in her bedroom, watching a magpie hopping around the garden.

'I heard that when you see a magpie on its own it isn't unlucky for you, it is just unlucky for the magpie because they don't have a friend. So I hope you are lucky and find a friend soon,' Maya said out loud, looking through the glass and out at the handsome black and white bird. Even though he was in the garden, he tilted his head as if he had heard her, and gave a little hop.

'I'm feeling lonely too, Magpie,' said Maya. 'My big sister Lauren is going away to university, and today is her last day at home. I am going to miss her SO much.'

Somehow it helped, saying it out loud. The bird came nearer, looking up at her as if he could understand what she was saying.

'Dad and Penny and Lauren are rushing around, packing up the car and charging up and down the stairs with bags and lamps and things,' Maya went on. 'I'm just getting in the way, and I don't want Lauren to see me feeling sad. She is so excited.'

Maya went over to the pot of peanuts she kept for the garden birds, and then opened the window to get the bird feeder she had stuck on the glass, and topped it up. Instead of being scared by the window opening, the magpie hopped even closer.

'You're beautiful,' said Maya.

Maya loved birds. Her room was full of pictures of them. She had a bird mobile over her bed, binoculars for bird spotting, and lots of books and DVDs about them. Her pencil case had birds on it, her pyjamas and nighties had birds on them, and even the clock on her bedroom wall played a different bird call every hour during the day. Luckily it switched off at night!

One good thing about having a ground- floor room was that Maya could see the garden birds really well. As well as the bird feeder on the window, there was a bird table right outside. She had already put out fat balls for the birds, because the migrating birds needed to build up energy before their long flight south. Maya knew which birds migrated and which visited or stayed over winter; she knew what special food each type of bird ate, and she spent lots of her pocket money on treats for them.

There was a knock at the door.

'Maya, can I come in?' came Lauren's voice.

'Yes,' said Maya, trying to sound more

cheerful than she felt. She knew that Lauren was so happy to be going away to university, and she wanted to be glad for her, but she couldn't help feeling that nothing was going to be the same any more. Lauren was the best big sister ever.

'Hey, Maya, are you OK?' said Lauren, coming in holding something behind her back.

Maya smiled and nodded, but a big tear escaped and rolled down her cheek.

'Oh Maya—don't cry!' said Lauren. She quickly hid something behind the curtain and went over to Maya to give her a big hug. 'I'll be back before you know it. And I've even got a ground-floor room, like you, so it will be easy for you to visit. It looks onto the university lake, so we'll be able to watch the birds together. I think there might be ducks!'

Maya laughed. Lauren was always showing her funny videos of ducks, and Maya had drawn a duck on Lauren's good luck card. Maya loved drawing birds.

'Now, close your eyes and put out your hands,' said Lauren.

Maya put out her hands and felt

something heavy and flat being put on them. She opened her eyes and saw it was just a simple, brown leather satchel.

'Open it,' said Lauren, smiling.

Maya looked inside the bag and took out what was there. She gasped. It was the most beautiful book she had ever seen. The cover was made from a deep-blue cloth with tiny gold birds all over it, and in gold lettering the title said *The Magical Kingdom of Birds*. There were pictures of birds all over the cover, back and front: birds in trees, in forests, in gardens; birds flying over the sea, soaring over mountaintops, diving into rivers; in deserts, in snow; birds in palaces and birds in cottages. Each picture was wonderful in its detail, and the birds were of all different shapes and sizes. Maya had the strangest feeling when she looked at each tiny scene, that it was getting bigger as she gazed at it. It was almost as if she was zooming in on it, like when she looked through her binoculars. She blinked and the pictures went back to normal, but Maya had a funny feeling inside, a feeling that something amazing was going to happen.

She opened the book. The first page had a detailed picture in black and white, of a very proud-looking magpie standing in a woodland clearing.

'It's a colouring book!' said Lauren. 'There are some special colouring pencils to go with it in the bag too. Look, there is something written inside the front cover.'

Maya looked away from the picture of the magpie to the writing.

To the Keeper of this book— it's time for you to visit the magical Kingdom waiting within. Believe in yourself—that will give you wings to fly!

'It's amazing!' said Maya. 'Where did you get it?'

'From Mum,' said Lauren. 'She gave it to me.'

'Oh Lauren—you can't give it to me, if Mum gave it to you,' said Maya, feeling sad. She wished she could remember her mum the way Lauren could. She had only been little when their mum had died.

'No—you don't understand,' said Lauren. 'Mum gave it to me, with the bag and the pencils, when she was ill and you were a toddler. She said to put it aside safely until you were older, so I put it at the back of my wardrobe. I was just sorting out things for university and felt like now was the right time to give it to you. I hadn't even opened it until today. It's beautiful, isn't it? It's amazing that Mum gave you a bird book when you were a baby, and you know so much about birds!'

'I know!' said Maya. She didn't expect to suddenly feel so happy and excited. Penny was the best stepmother anyone could have, but it was special to know that her mum had been thinking of her, and had got her this book when she was just a baby. How had her mum known she would grow up loving birds so much?

This sad day was turning to something new and wonderful, and Maya knew, deep down, that it was somehow because of this special book.

There was a tap on the window. The magpie was now perched on the back of the garden seat, so that he was really close to the glass.

'Cheeky thing!' laughed Lauren. 'Look, I'll be back later. Sorry we're rushing around so much. I thought you might like to start colouring in a picture while you're waiting. Dad's taking us all out to dinner once the car is packed.'

Lauren left Maya with the book and the bag and the pencils, and Maya hugged the book to her chest.

'Thanks, Mum,' she whispered.

She went to her table by the window. The magpie was still looking in at her.

'Look, there's a big picture of you on the very first page,' she said, holding it up to the window for the magpie to see. 'I wonder what other birds are in it.' She turned the pages. Oddly they were all blank, and, odder still, the book itself kept flicking back to the first page, as if it didn't want her to go any further.

'This is a strange colouring book,' said Maya.

The magpie tapped the glass again. He gazed at her with his shiny black eyes and put his head on one side. Maya had the funniest feeling that both the book and the magpie were telling her to 'get on with it'.

'Well, I won't have to worry about colouring you in wrong!' She laughed. 'You can be my model if you stay still.'

The magpie hopped up and down on the spot, but didn't fly off. He seemed to be watching her.

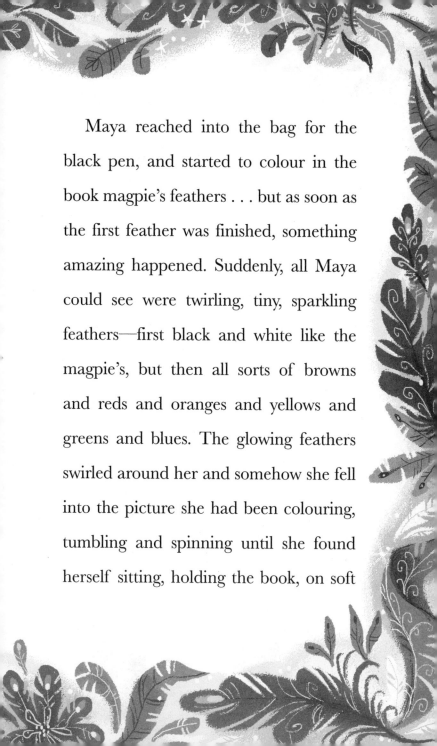

Maya reached into the bag for the black pen, and started to colour in the book magpie's feathers . . . but as soon as the first feather was finished, something amazing happened. Suddenly, all Maya could see were twirling, tiny, sparkling feathers—first black and white like the magpie's, but then all sorts of browns and reds and oranges and yellows and greens and blues. The glowing feathers swirled around her and somehow she fell into the picture she had been colouring, tumbling and spinning until she found herself sitting, holding the book, on soft green moss in a woodland glade. Next to her was the magpie, now much taller than her. Looking at the flowers and plants around her, Maya could see that it wasn't the magpie who had got bigger, but she who had got smaller.

'It worked! It really worked!' cried a voice, and Maya turned to see a little fairy emerge from underneath a bush. 'The Keeper of the Book has come at last!'

Collect them all!

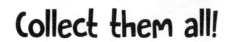

Magical kingdom of Birds
The Sleepy Hummingbirds

ANNE BOOTH
Illustrated by Rosie Butcher

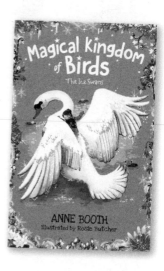

Magical kingdom of Birds
The Ice Swans

ANNE BOOTH
Illustrated by Rosie Butcher

Magical kingdom of Birds
The Missing Fairy-Wrens

ANNE BOOTH
Illustrated by Rosie Butcher

Ready for more great stories?

Kitty and the Sky Garden Adventure

Girl by day. Cat by night. Ready for adventure.
Written by Paula Harrison • Illustrated by Jenny Løvlie

Written by Gill Lewis

Willow Wildthing and the Swamp Monster

Illustrated by Rebecca Bagley

FREDDIE'S AMAZING BAKERY

THE COOKIE MYSTERY

Written by HARRIET WHITEHORN
Illustrated by ALEX G GRIFFITHS

ISADORA MOON Goes on Holiday

Half vampire, half fairy, totally unique!
Harriet Muncaster